MOUSE WAS MAD

Linda Urban

Illustrated by Henry Cole

Harcourt Children's Books Houghton Mifflin Harcourt New York 2009

Requests for permission to make copies of any part of
the work should be submitted online at
www.harcourt.com/contact or mailed to the
following address: Permissions Department,
Houghton Mifflin Harcourt Publishing Company,
6277 Sea Harbor Drive, Orlando, Florida 32887-6777.

Harcourt Children's Books is an imprint of
Houghton Mifflin Harcourt Publishing Company.

www.hmhbooks.com

Library of Congress Cataloging-in-Publication Data
Urban, Linda.
Mouse was mad/Linda Urban; [illustrator] Henry Cole.
p.   cm.
Summary: Mouse struggles to find the right way to
express his anger, modeling the behavior of Hare, Bear,
Hedgehog, and Bobcat, only to discover that his own way
may be the best way of all.
[1. Anger—Fiction. 2. Individuality—Fiction. 3. Mice—Fiction.
4. Animals—Fiction.] I. Cole, Henry, 1955- ill. II. Title.
PZ7.U637Mo 2009
[E]—dc22   2007045081 \
ISBN 978-0-15-205337-6

First edition
H G F E D C B A

Printed in Singapore

The illustrations in this book were done in
watercolor, colored pencil, and ink on Arches hot press
watercolor paper.
The display type was set in Typography of Coop Black.
The text type was set in Billy.
Color separations by Colourscan Co. Pte. Ltd., Singapore
Printed and bound by Tien Wah Press, Singapore
Production supervision by Christine Witnik
Designed by Michele Wetherbee

For Claire and Jack—L. U.

For my pals Anita and Debbie,
with affection—H. C.

Mouse was mad. **Hopping mad.**

"You look ridiculous," said Hare.
Mouse stopped hopping.

"Let me show you how to hop properly," said Hare,
who truly was a hopping whiz.

Mouse tried to hop like Hare.
Nothing doing.

Mouse

hop-hop-flopped—

SPLISH!—

into a mucky mud puddle.

Now Mouse was really mad.
Stomping mad.

"You call that stomping?" said Bear.

Mouse stopped stomping.

"Stomping, done right, should result in the shaking of trees
and the rumbling of earth," said Bear. Bear stomped.

The trees shook, the earth rumbled.

Mouse tried to stomp like Bear.

The trees did not shake.

The earth did not rumble.

Mouse

stomp-stomp-flomped—

SPLUSH!—

into another mucky mud puddle.

Now Mouse was really, really mad.
Screaming mad.

"That's hardly a scream at all," said Bobcat.
Mouse stopped screaming.

"When I scream, you can hear it echo through the woods."
Bobcat screamed to prove his point. It echoed and echoed.

Mouse opened his mouth wide and let out
the loudest scream he could manage.
No echo.

He tried arching his back like Bobcat

but lost his balance and fell—

SPLOSH!—

into yet another mucky mud puddle.

Now Mouse was really, really, really mad.

Rolling-around-on-the-ground mad.

"Pull your feet in," said Hedgehog.

Mouse stopped rolling.

"The best rolling is achieved when the body is a perfect sphere." Hedgehog tucked in his nose and his feet and his hands. He was a perfect sphere.

Mouse tucked in his nose and his feet and his hands.

He was not a perfect sphere, but he was close.

He pulled in his tail

and rolled around and around—

SPLOOSH!—

into the muckiest mud puddle of all.

Now Mouse was really, really, really, really mad.
Standing-still mad.

Mouse did not hop. He did not stomp.

He did not scream or roll on the ground.

He stood very, very still.

"Impressive," said Hare.
"What control," said Bear.
"Are you breathing?"
asked Hedgehog.

Mouse took a deep breath.

He let his breath out.

Bobcat heard air whistle through Mouse's nose,

but he did not see Mouse move.

"Inspiring," said Bobcat.

Bobcat stood very still. He breathed deep and tried not to move.

"Your ears twitched," said Hare.
"Let me try." But he could not keep
his tail from wiggling.

Bear tried, but when he breathed deep, trees moved and the ground shook a little. Hedgehog came closest, but even he could not keep his bristles from bristling.

They stood together for a long time, breathing and trying to be still.

And then, Mouse realized he was no longer mad.

"I feel better now," said Mouse.

"You look better now," said Bear.

"But you need a bath," said Hedgehog.

"Good idea," said Mouse.

SPLASH!

A MICHAEL NEUGEBAUER BOOK

NORTH-SOUTH BOOKS / NEW YORK / LONDON

How Will We Get to the Beach?

BRIGITTE LUCIANI
ILLUSTRATED BY
EVE THARLET
TRANSLATED BY
ROSEMARY LANNING

One beautiful summer
day Roxanne decided to
go to the beach.
Everything she wanted to
take with her could be
counted on the fingers
of one hand.

the turtle,
the umbrella,
the thick book
of stories,
the ball, and,
of course, her baby.

But the car wouldn't start.

"Then we'll take the bus to the beach," said Roxanne.

But something couldn't go
with them. What was it?

The little green turtle!

Animals weren't allowed on the bus.
"We can't go to the beach without the turtle!"
cried Roxanne.

"Then we'll ride our bike to the beach," she said.

But something couldn't go with them. What was it?

The orange-spotted ball!

The ball wouldn't fit on the bicycle.
"We can't go to the beach without the ball!"
cried Roxanne.

"Then we'll ride our skateboard to the beach," she said.

But something couldn't go with them. What was it?

The big yellow umbrella.

Roxanne didn't have a free hand to hold it.
"We can't go to the beach without the umbrella!"
cried Roxanne.

"Then we'll ride our kayak to the beach," she said.

But something couldn't go with them. What was it?

The thick blue book of stories.

The kayak was very wobbly, and the book might get wet.
"We can't go to the beach without the book!"
 cried Roxanne.

"Then we'll fly in a balloon to the beach,"
she said.

But something couldn't go with them.
What was it?

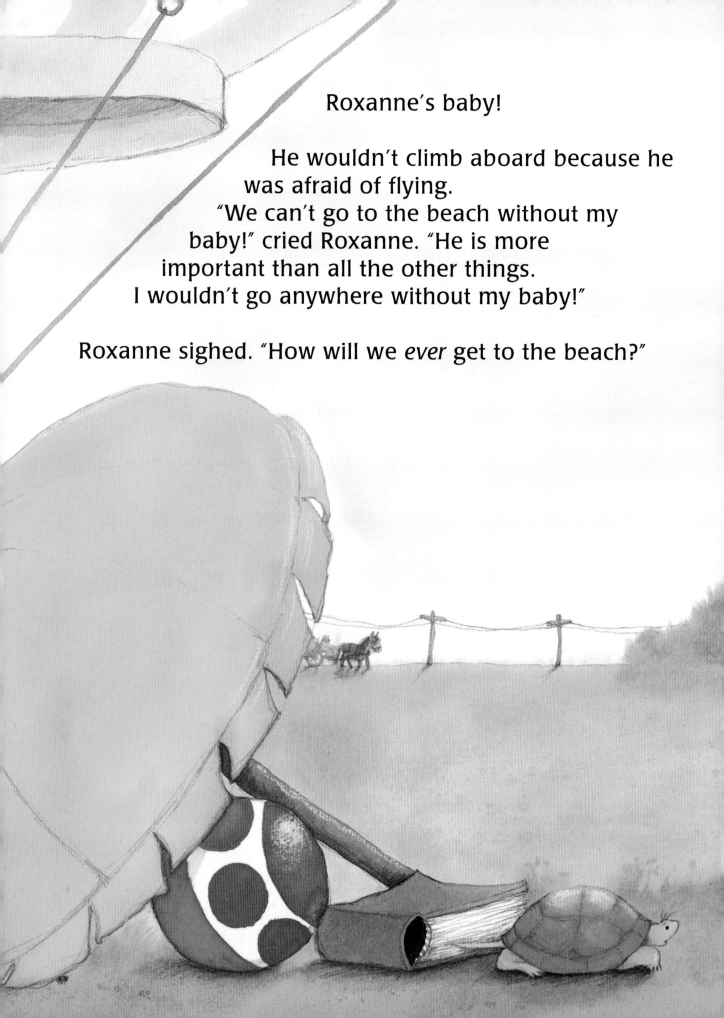

Roxanne's baby!

He wouldn't climb aboard because he was afraid of flying.
"We can't go to the beach without my baby!" cried Roxanne. "He is more important than all the other things. I wouldn't go anywhere without my baby!"

Roxanne sighed. "How will we *ever* get to the beach?"

Just then a farmer passed by with his horse and cart.
He was on his way to the beach to sell cherries.

So they piled aboard:
Roxanne,
the green turtle,
the big yellow umbrella,
the thick blue book of stories,
the orange-spotted ball,
and, of course, her baby.

And they had a wonderful time!